Officer Belamy travels to a tiny island on the Norwegian coast to help clear up the murder of a French citizen.

The island offers an awful boat ride, tall, blond Norwegian police officers, and a talkative lady desperate for company.

And silence. Lots of silence.

R.W. WALLACE

Author of the Ghost Detective Series

A search for solitude
only works if your
neighbors play along

TWO'S COMPANY

A Mystery Short Story

Two's Company

by R.W. Wallace

Copyright © 2019 by R.W. Wallace

Cover by the author

Copy edit by Jinxie Gervasio

Cover Illustration 951340 © Steve Johnson | pexels.com

All characters and events in this book, other than those clearly in the public domain, are fictitious and any resemblance to real persons, living or dead, is purely coincidental.

All rights reserved. No part of this publication may be reproduced, distributed, or transmitted in any form or by any means, including photocopying, recording, or other electronic or mechanical methods, without the prior written permission of the publisher, except in the case of brief quotations embodied in critical reviews and certain other noncommercial uses permitted by copyright law. For permission requests, write to the publisher, addressed "Attention: Permissions Coordinator," at the address below.

www.rwwallace.com

ISBN: [979-10-95707-27-1]

Main category—Fiction

Other category—Mystery

First Edition

Also by R.W. Wallace

Mystery

The Tolosa Mystery Series
The Red Brick Haze (free)
The Red Brick Cellars

Ghost Detective Shorts (coming soon)
Just Desserts
Lost Friends
Family Bonds
Till Death
Common Ground

Short Stories
Hidden Horrors
Critters
Gertrude and the Trojan Horse
First Impressions
Let Them Eat Cake
Out of Sight
Two's Company

Science Fiction (short stories)
The Vanguard
Quarantine (Lollapalooza)
Common Enemies (Lollapalooza)

Adventure (short stories)
Size Matters

Urban Fantasy (short stories)
Unexpected Consequences

TWO'S COMPANY

I was in hell and it was full of water.

The bow of the tiny fishing boat tipped up, and the stern—carrying me with it—bowed down. The spray of a cut wave jumped over the gunwale starboard side, washed the cluttered deck, and disappeared overboard port-side.

I was pretty sure it washed over me, too, but I was too focused on my own misery to notice.

Inside the cockpit, my guide—a tall stalk of a man named Gunnar—turned to make sure I was still there, shaking his head. He stood there, all dry and comfortable, next to our skipper—a retired fisherman with aviator glasses that I was pretty sure he must have owned for at least thirty years, orange fisherman overalls and a knitted jacket, and boots that looked sturdy enough to withstand a storm.

According to my guide, this was *not* a storm. It was *a breeze*.

I was never getting on a boat ever again.

Nor accepting the cases of Frenchmen getting killed abroad, no matter how tempting the destination.

It started out all right in the harbor, with the boat rocking just the tiniest little bit. My stomach wasn't happy, even then, but it had just been a vague feeling of, *okay, this isn't particularly fun*. Enough for me to decide to stay outside while the skipper and Gunnar took to the cockpit, probably laughing at the foreign woman with the weak stomach.

From there, it only got worse. Once we cleared the harbor, we took the full blast of the…breeze. I wouldn't be able to describe our surroundings to save my life, as my entire focus was on the deck, my feet, my stomach. I had tunnel vision, not registering a single thing going on outside of the confines of the fishing boat.

The only thought in my head was, *do not throw up, do not throw up*.

Somehow—miraculously—I survived.

The skipper lined us up next to the docks of the small island that was our destination. Well, below it would be a more accurate description, since I had to climb up a large, mossy ladder to reach the actual dock which loomed over the little fishing boat.

"I know Norwegians are tall," I muttered as I climbed, "but this must be out of proportion even for them."

"It's low tide," Gunnar said from a mile above me on the dock. "At high tide, you wouldn't need the ladder at all." His accent was strong, but easy to understand. Like all the other Norwegians I'd met so far, he pronounced every syllable, said "de ting" instead of "the thing," and sounded like he spoke Norwegian and not English if you didn't listen to the actual words.

"Ah," I said as I enjoyed standing on a non-moving surface and took a deep, refreshing breath. "I do not live by the ocean. Rivers do not have tides."

Gunnar grinned at me, showing off white, but crooked teeth. "I guess you will want to change before we see the crime scene?"

I hesitated. After two long flights, a stressful hour of running through the airport in Frankfurt, and a three-hour drive to the dreaded harbor, I wanted to see what I'd come here to see. But I was soaked through from the waist down and my feet made squishy noises in my shoes every time I took a step.

"A quick change of clothes would not be unwelcome," I said. "Thank you." I also realized that though my stomach was already feeling more perky, my mind was still sluggish. A couple of extra minutes before seeing where my countryman was killed wouldn't hurt.

Fifteen minutes later, I walked up to a wide, white-painted wooden house that stood at what apparently passed for a crossroads on this island—meaning two of the island's three paths met right in front of the living room window.

"The island has three quad bikes and one museum-worthy tractor," Gunnar explained as we walked. I kept some distance between us to avoid getting a crick in my neck from looking up at him. "So far, we haven't felt the need to borrow any of them since the house is so close to the docks."

As we rounded the house, I was treated to the view of a cute rose garden and a terrace at the back. All six available chairs were filled by sturdy police officers in uniform, four men and two women, pouring over notes and pictures.

"Officer Bellamy," Gunnar said. "Let me introduce my team." He gave me the names of his officers and their specialty. Four were local officers from the police station only a boat ride and an hour's drive away, while two were specialists brought in from Trondheim, the same city I'd been through earlier.

"Bellamy is from France," Gunnar explained. "She'll bring her own expertise, of course, but she can also help us if there's any French involved anywhere, she can talk to the victim's family and friends, and might help if there's any cultural context we're missing."

Most importantly, I was there so both parties could prove that we were cooperating. That the Norwegians weren't hiding anything from the French, and that France took it very seriously when one of her citizens was killed abroad.

Gunnar led the way through the front door into a dark hallway. It smelled of old house, salt, and death. "The body isn't here anymore, of course," he said. "We couldn't keep it for two days with the state it was already in."

"I understand." I'd seen the pictures. "Do you know when he died?" The first estimation had been between ten and fifteen days, which left too large a window.

"Yes," Gunnar said. He held the door open for me to enter the kitchen before him. "It happened on the weekend of the first of May."

I stopped to meet his gaze. "And you're not happy about that because…"

Gunnar sighed. "This island is basically deserted until the summer vacation starts. Except on long weekends."

"Then how many people were here at the time of the murder?"

"Nine families." He crossed his arms over his chest and leaned against the kitchen counter. "Instead of just one person."

"One?"

Gunnar nodded his head to the path outside. "This island has only one permanent resident, a Mrs. Hoftun two houses down."

"*Bon*," I said. "With only one suspect, you would not have needed me to cross half a continent to lend a hand."

Gunnar chuckled. "True. And Mrs. Hoftun is more the grandmotherly type than a cold-blooded murderer, so that might have posed a different type of problem."

I looked around at the kitchen. "This is where he was found?"

White Formica counters ran down two walls, with matching overhead cabinets and a small table in front of the window. It all looked like it came straight out of the sixties. The sun shone through the sheer white curtains, illuminating the single chair as if it contained a revelation.

Gunnar pointed to the chair. "He'd been sitting there, eating breakfast. There was rat poison in the cereal, so once that did its thing, he ended up on the floor right here."

I eyed the window. "Why did nobody see him? The path cannot be more than a meter away from the window."

Gunnar tilted his head from side to side. "You see someone sitting on the chair. Someone lying on the floor, not so much." He met my eyes as he continued. "We did the test, and it is possible to see someone lying on the floor, but you have to step all the way up to the window and look for him. Which is how Mrs. Hoftun discovered he was dead."

"Ah. She is one of those."

With half a grin, Gunnar stepped up to the window to look outside. "Don't be too quick to judge. It's a very small community here. If you can even call it that when the entire island has only two inhabitants. She was used to him being a recluse, but not dropping out of view for two whole weeks. So, yes, she went looking for him, out of concern."

"He was a recluse?" This didn't match with the information I'd gathered before leaving home.

"Yes," Gunnar replied. "He was apparently an author who came here to be alone and write. He paid one of the local fishermen to take him grocery shopping every two weeks, and went on daily walks to the cairn, but other than that, he stayed in this house."

I shuddered at the thought of getting into a boat every two weeks.

"Maybe he was a recluse because his only other option was to talk with Mrs. Hoftun," I said.

Gunnar shook his head. "Even when the island was full of people—that's about a maximum of twenty-five, by the way—he stayed by himself. He was becoming famous for it. The eccentric Frenchman." He shrugged as if to apologize for insulting my countryman. "What do you know about him?"

"*Bon.*" I had trouble making my two narratives match in my head. Perhaps saying it out loud would help.

I brought out my notes on my phone, for backup, though I knew everything by heart. "Jérôme Lenotre was thirty-nine years old and from Lyon. He grew up in the city, studied there, and worked there as an engineer for fifteen years. He loved skiing, but other than that, his activities centered around a big city life.

Theater, clubbing, cinema, restaurants with friends. He was part of a karate club for almost ten years.

"The day he turned thirty-nine, he walked into the office of his boss and resigned. He did the three months to finish his contract, then left the country—to come stay here."

I powered down my phone and put my hands on my hips. "Everybody agrees he was an extrovert and social person."

Gunnar's gaze was still on the ocean outside. "Maybe he needed some time by himself. Return to nature."

He must have seen my skepticism. "It's a thing, you know," he said. "It's why all Norwegians dream to have a holiday home like this." He waved to encompass the house. "To get away from the stress and noise of the city. Get some peace. Remember that nature is bigger and more important than us."

"Hmm." I idly opened and closed the cupboards as I talked. There were tons of canned goods, some breads that seemed to be of the half-baked kind, and some fresh produce that was well on its way to becoming compost.

"Norwegians might like to mix nature and city," I said. "But the French do not. You are either a city person, who will go to the mountains from time to time to ski or hike, but get back home to the teeming city life by the end of the day, or you are a country bumpkin who gets lost whenever you have to change metros. Jérôme Lenotre was a city boy, through and through."

Gunnar shrugged. "Might look like he changed."

One of the officers from outside popped his head through the door to say something to Gunnar in Norwegian.

"We're done here for today, I'm afraid," he translated. "I'm sorry you didn't get to see any more today, but the fun will in any case start tomorrow."

"Why?"

He flashed a large smile. "Monday is the seventeenth of May, our Constitution Day. It means this is another long weekend where most of the people who own the houses on this island will come. We'll have lots of suspects to interview."

Well, that was something, at least.

But… "You are not staying on the island during the investigation?" My stomach was *not* happy with the idea of getting back on a boat so soon.

"Oh, no," Gunnar said, his eyebrows raising toward his receding hairline. "There's not enough housing for us. This house is basically the only one that's open for rent. And most of my team wants to go home to their families tonight."

"Of course. Of course." God, I really didn't want to get back on that boat. And *again* tomorrow morning.

Gunnar held onto the door knob, but didn't open the door. "If you're not easily spooked by a recent murder, I'm sure we could arrange for you to sleep here tonight. There are three more bedrooms in addition to the one used by our victim."

I hesitated. I didn't want to come off as weak, but throwing up in front of the entire team wouldn't exactly make me appear strong.

"I will take you up on that offer," I said. "I have had a long day, and it will allow me to see the island and catch up with your team."

"Excellent." Gunnar opened the door and yelled something in Norwegian to the group out back. "Erik will show you the room and the facilities. We'll be back here tomorrow, probably a little after nine."

And thus, I found myself all alone in a large house smelling of antiseptic with an undercurrent of death, on an island with only one other inhabitant.

☙

At first, the silence was deafening.

This place had *nothing*. No cars, no motorbikes—hell, no bikes, even—no people yelling, no sirens howling.

Nothing.

As I stood on the path in front of the house after having two different kinds of canned food for dinner, all I could hear were a couple of birds chirping and the breeze rustling through the trees.

I was actually thankful for the small alder trees covering the island. Whenever there was the slightest hint of wind, their leaves moved and made a whirring sound. I felt like it was the only thing proving I hadn't gone deaf.

Gunnar had explained how to get to the cairn before leaving. It was apparently *the* cairn, the spot marking the highest point on the island, at a whopping thirty-six meters above sea-level.

I might be a city girl, but Lyon had more height difference than that just in the city center.

I took off down the grass-covered path, found the next "intersection," where I turned right, and climbed the tiny ascent to the cairn.

The cairn stood a head taller than me and was as wide as it was tall. A ladder leaned against one side, allowing for visitors climb it if they wanted.

It really was the highest point for quite some distance in all directions, so the breeze was a lot stronger than it had been in front of the house. I stayed to the West of the cairn, seeking what shelter I could find.

To the East, mountains rose into pink clouds, tall and imposing. To the South, there seemed to be some *really* flat island covered in windmills. The North was basically more islands like the one I was standing on.

The West held nothing but water. I'd checked out the map, and once you cleared this small group of islands, it was straight into the North Sea, with Iceland as the next stop.

A lonely lighthouse stood as the last outpost on an island maybe a couple of kilometers West, a last guardian before the big blue.

The sun hung just above the tip of the lighthouse, a heavy mix of orange and pink, ready to plunge into the sea. I decided to stay to watch the sun set. It's not like I had anywhere I had to be, with a house without TV, no internet, no people to please.

I actually had the time to just sit here.

I slid down with my back to the cairn and snapped a couple of photos before shoving my phone back in my pocket. It felt like blasphemy to use modern technology in a place like this.

I was just coming to the realization that Gunnar might have been right about our victim having converted from city boy to country boy when I heard steps approaching.

A little old lady who was even shorter than me, with wispy white hair and thick glasses, cleared the knoll on the other side of the cairn.

"*Neimmen, hallo*," she said with a huge smile.

"Hello," I replied. "I assume you are Mrs. Hoftun?" I prayed the woman spoke English, or this would become a very tiresome conversation.

"Why, yes, that's me!" She beamed. She was missing several teeth, but the ones she had left seemed to be in good condition. "I saw you walk past my house earlier and thought I'd introduce myself."

Okay, her English would not be a problem. She had less of an accent than Gunnar.

"I'm Officer Belamy," I said, extending a hand for her to shake.

She had a firm grip. Once she released my hand, she sat down next to me.

Though I'd complained about the silence earlier, I now found myself oddly annoyed that she intruded on my solitude. I'd started to hear myself think, which was a nice change from my everyday life.

"You're here because of poor Jérôme?" Mrs. Hoftun asked. "That poor boy. Never bothered anyone and now he's gone. I certainly hope someone else will come and rent the house now, I so enjoyed having someone else on the island with me."

"How long have you lived here?" I asked.

"Oh." She raised her hands to her cheeks as if the question flustered her. "I've lived here all my life. Born and raised in that house. Imagine I'll die in it, too."

I eyed the sun to gauge how long until it set, but though it had moved past the lighthouse, it was far from reaching the horizon.

"You have not always been alone on the island, I assume?"

"Oh, no," Mrs. Hoftun replied. "In the fifties, all the houses were filled with families. Kids from the other islands came here to go to our school. It was quite busy, I assure you." She smoothed down a crease in her pants. "But these days, all the jobs are in the city. Even the fishermen can't make a living out here anymore. So one by one, the people left. Now, the houses are in use only during vacations—which is better than standing empty all year 'round, I guess."

"Did you talk often with Jérôme?"

Mrs. Hoftun sighed. "Not as often as I'd have liked. He was always searching for silence. It helped him find his stories, he said. So I chatted at him as long as he'd let me and tried to make do."

"I assume it can get lonely out here." I wondered if perhaps there was an equilibrium to find between refreshing solitude and crushing loneliness.

"Oh, yes," Mrs. Hoftun replied and folded her hands in her lap. "I do enjoy my own company, of course, but there's only so much one can do with only a radio for feedback." A sigh. "I had such high hopes when I heard that house had been rented for the whole winter. I didn't plan to bother him every day, of course, but I must admit to being somewhat disappointed when he turned out to be all but a hermit."

I studied the woman's profile. Her lips were turned down in disappointment and her forehead folded into a frown.

"Was he rude to you in any way?" I asked her. Perhaps if the guy was the classic Frenchman who didn't speak the language and therefore came off as rude, it could explain why someone decided to kill him.

"Oh, no," Mrs. Hoftun replied. "He was perfectly polite. But it was still quite obvious when he'd had enough and wanted to be alone with his writing. It usually didn't take more than five minutes."

I surreptitiously checked my watch. Five minutes sounded about right. I wouldn't mind some alone time myself.

Mrs. Hoftun launched into an explanation of the creation of the cairn, and the path leading up to it, and the floating docks in front of her house.

It was half past eleven and the sun was still not setting. It kept crawling toward the East, but vertically there didn't seem to be much movement. The sky sported a magnificent canvas of colors; white and clear blue at the top, purple and orange in the middle, and indigo mixed with red just below the sun's current position. I could get used to watching this every night.

"When does the sun set?" I asked. How long would I have to listen to her chatter before I could fall face-down in my bed and finally rest after such a long day of traveling?

"Oh. You want to watch it set?" Mrs. Hoftun's eyes widened. "That might take a while, dear. I think the sun dips below the horizon for an hour or so at this time of the year, but it's not for another hour, at least."

Huh. Geography lessons from my youth made a reluctant reappearance. "How close are we to the arctic circle?"

"Three hundred kilometers, perhaps?"

I let my head fall into my hands. It never got dark at night. What kind of a fairy tale place was this?

Mrs. Hoftun rambled happily on, not needing much input from me. After thirty minutes, I gave up, and excused myself to go to bed.

She tried to invite herself over for breakfast the next morning, but I pretended not to understand her and took off before she found a way to reformulate her request.

ଓ

After my breakfast of dry biscuits and coffee the next morning, Gunnar walked through the door accompanied by seven colleagues. Half of them, including Gunnar, had to bend down to pass the kitchen door.

"We'll divide the different inhabitants between us as they arrive," he said. "We'll interview everyone, even the ones who weren't here for the weekend when the murder happened."

I nodded my agreement. I shook hands with everyone but remembered no names. They were all guttural and German-sounding and belonged to tall, blonde people.

I faced Gunnar, deciding I'd just use him as my main contact during my stay. "What do you know of the rat poison that was used? Can that lead us anywhere?"

"Doubtful," Gunnar replied. "It's the type of thing that everyone has in their basement somewhere. We even found one in this house. We'll ask everyone to hand over theirs when we do the interviews, in the hopes to find a match, but I'm not keeping my hopes up."

A face popped up outside the kitchen window. I jumped, then realized it was just Mrs. Hoftun with a big smile.

"*Mon Dieu*," I murmured. "Does she never stop?"

Gunnar chuckled. "Don't judge her too hard. She's out here all alone all year. It must be exciting for her to see so many people at once."

"I am not certain I like your silver lining," I said, but conceded a smile.

We all moved outside to divide the island's inhabitants between us. Gunnar gave me the Hansen family, who should arrive shortly, and who owned three houses, including the one we were standing in.

"Would you mind asking Mrs. Hoftun to walk you down to their house?" Gunnar asked. "I hate being rude to her, but I don't want her overhearing me giving instructions to my team."

"And how do I get rid of her so I can talk to the Hansens?"

Gunnar flashed a smile at me, making him appear ten years younger. "Aren't you French famous for being rude? I'm sure you'll think of something. Or, if everything else fails, you can push her in the water."

Eyes narrowed, I walked across the terrace to meet Mrs. Hoftun around the corner. "Ha, ha," I said. "Maybe I will do just that and tell her it was your idea."

I left the team chuckling at my expense, but found I quite enjoyed it. Not to mention the picture of Mrs. Hoftun in the water. If she'd lived here her entire life, she'd know how to swim, right?

We were meeting the Hansens on the dock where I'd arrived the day before. Apparently, it belonged to them, and they were the ones fixing up the old boathouse at the end of the dock. Mrs. Hansen thought it would be very pretty once it was done and hoped it would draw more families to spend more time on the island.

The walk took only five minutes, but by the time we reached the docks, I knew everything there was to know about the families on this side of the island. She promised to tell me about the ones from the North later. Joy.

To hear Mrs. Hoftun talk, I'd imagined the Hansen family to arrive in a yacht, but no. They arrived in a fishing boat much like the one I'd traveled with yesterday.

The father of the family, a bald gentleman in his late seventies, wore full fisherman paraphernalia, including the enormous boots. His wife looked dressed to go on a fancy dinner in town, with neat trousers, a button-down blouse, and a ton of makeup.

A second couple occupied the stern. Mrs. Hoftun explained the woman was one of the daughters of the Hansen family, and the man was her husband.

I introduced myself quickly once the family disembarked. They all looked suitably serious when they realized I was there because of the murder and asked if we'd found the culprit yet.

When Mrs. Hoftun started chatting with Mrs. Hansen, I saw an opportunity. "Solveig, Thomas," I said, addressing the younger couple. "Would you mind going inside with me to talk for a few minutes?"

Solveig's glance in Mrs. Hoftun's direction showed how transparent I was. "Sure," she said with a smile. "Come inside. I need to turn on the water and electricity anyway."

Two's Company

They talked about life on the island and its inhabitants while they opened the house up for the weekend. They were in the middle of fixing the house up, and it looked like it would be a little piece of paradise once it was finished. It even had a wall-to-ceiling window straight onto the water.

They hadn't known Jérôme Lenotre too well, but they'd liked what they saw. He'd paid six months rent up front, never had any parties the neighbors could complain about, cut the grass on the path like they'd asked him to, and clearly adhered to the philosophy of the area—meaning, respecting nature and appreciating the luxury of the quiet.

I really didn't get the feeling that these two were my killers. First, because the profile just didn't fit. Second, because they had no motive. They'd lost an income source and renting out a house where there'd been a murder might not be all that easy out here.

"We've already put out a notice to search for new tenants," Solveig explained. She waggled her eyebrows. "I wouldn't dare come out here and tell Mrs. Hoftun we weren't working on it."

"I quite understand," I replied with a wink. "Now, before I leave. I am afraid I will have to ask you if I can take your rat poison. I will need it to run some tests."

"Rat poison?" Solveig shook her head. "Nobody out here's going to have rat poison. There's never been any rats."

My heart sped up as the importance of this statement hit me. "No rats?"

Solveig spread her hands. "How would they get here? I know rats can probably swim, but not several hundred meters in one go. And the small boats that come here don't have vermin, either."

"The only animals on this island," Thomas said, "are a couple of deer who survived the swim from the mainland and some annoying mink. I've never even seen a mouse."

I thanked them for their time and left, my head spinning.

☙

THE HOUSE WAS empty when I made it back after a discussion with the older Hansens and using the "rude Frenchman" thing to get rid of Mrs. Hoftun. I left a note for Gunnar on the kitchen table and went back to the cairn.

I had a feeling I'd be leaving before the day was over, and I wanted to enjoy the silence one more time first.

The wind felt nourishing. Like every little gust went straight to my lungs, and from there throughout my body, giving life to every last muscle.

I felt like I hadn't drawn a really deep breath in years.

I wouldn't trade my life in a big city for this on a permanent basis, like Jérôme Lenotre had done. But as a yearly getaway? It sounded like a brilliant way to hear myself think and remember that there are larger forces at work in this world than us puny humans.

I don't know how long I sat there listening to the wind and smelling the sea on the air, but eventually a body sat down next to me.

I opened one eye and gave an uncharacteristically mellow smile. "I like your country, Gunnar."

"Why, thank you," he replied as he wound his arms around his knees. "I'm afraid this isn't quite representative of the entire country, though. We do have big cities and city folks, too."

We enjoyed the silence for a couple of minutes.

"Did you collect a lot of rat poison?" I asked finally.

"Nobody has any."

"*Ouais...*" My eyes had been tracking a tanker on the horizon for some time. It was placed exactly on the separation between sea and sky, making it look like a child's drawing, where the ship is *on* the water. Now it seemed to be sinking, with only the top half visible over the horizon.

"How long before you'll get feedback on the prints on the rat poison from the cellar?" I asked.

"Tonight," he replied. "Do you need any help booking your return flight?"

I sighed. "Not for me. But I'd appreciate the help with shipping the coffin." It was my main reason for being here, really, to accompany the body back home.

"I'll look into it."

A couple of seagulls cried to our left and were soon joined by at least twenty more. Someone had a successful fishing trip.

"So, Mrs. Hoftun, huh?" Gunnar said.

"*Ouais.*" I took a deep breath, feeling the ocean air all the way to my toes. "There is a point when solitude tips into loneliness. I am guessing Mrs. Hoftun tipped over years ago. Having a neighbor who was present but refused to interact with her must have been torture."

Gunnar leaned his forehead on his folded arms. "I don't see how killing him helps, though."

"I assume that she is somewhat beyond logic at this point. But it does open for the possibility of a new lodger, does it not?"

He sighed. "I guess it does." His head lifted and he bumped his shoulder into mine. "Maybe you would like to rent the house now it's available?"

I smiled at him. "Maybe I will."

༄

I DID THROW up on the trip back across the fjord, but nobody seemed to mind.

I shared the fishing boat with Gunnar and Mrs. Hoftun, on their way to the police station in Trondheim.

Mrs. Hoftun was the happiest future convict I'd ever seen, looking about her as if on her way to an adventure, asking Gunnar questions about the prison—how many inmates, what activities they had, what she had to do to avoid isolation.

To each their own.

I would bring poor Jérôme home and tell his parents justice would be served.

Then I'd drop by the pharmacy to see what they had for curing seasickness.

THANK YOU

THANK YOU FOR reading *Two's Company*. I hope you enjoyed it!

The setting for this story is completely stolen from the island where my family has a summer house. The nice inhabitants of the story, too. The murderer, not so much!

And there really are no rodents.

If you liked the story, you might want to check out some of my other books mentioned on the next page. It's mostly Mysteries, but a few other genres will pop up, too.

And don't forget that the first book of my *Tolosa Mystery* series, *The Red Brick Haze*, is available for free on my website.

R.W. Wallace
www.rwwallace.com

Also by R.W. Wallace

Mystery

The Tolosa Mystery Series
The Red Brick Haze (free)
The Red Brick Cellars
The Red Brick Basilica

Ghost Detective Shorts (coming soon)
Just Desserts
Lost Friends
Family Bonds
Till Death
Family History
Common Ground
Heritage
Eternal Bond
New Beginnings

Short Stories
Cold Blue Eternity
Hidden Horrors
Critters
Gertrude and the Trojan Horse
First Impressions
Let Them Eat Cake
Out of Sight
Two's Company
Like Mother Like Daughter

Fantasy (Short Stories)
Unexpected Consequences
Morbier Impossible
A Second Chance

Science Fiction (Short Stories)
The Vanguard

Lollapalooza Shorts
Quarantine
Common Enemies
Coiled Danger
Mars Meeting

Adventure (Short Stories)
Size Matters

www.ingramcontent.com/pod-product-compliance
Lightning Source LLC
LaVergne TN
LVHW041718060526
838201LV00043B/800